To Grace, Max & Benjy, Darcy & Rufus.

First U.S. edition 2016

Library of Congress Catalog Card Number pending
ISBN 978-0-7636-8926-1

16 17 18 19 20 21 APS 10 9 8 7 6 5 4 3 2 1

Printed in Humen, Dongguan, China

This book was typeset in Goudy Old Style.
The illustrations were done in colored pencils and pen.

Candlewick Press
99 Dover Street
Somerville, Massachusetts 02144

visit us at www.candlewick.com

MELTDOWN!

Jill Murphy

CANDLEWICK PRESS

One morning, Mom decided to take Roxy
grocery shopping.
"Roxy can help Mommy," said Mom.
"HELP MOMMY!" shouted Roxy,
jumping up and down with glee.

Then Roxy couldn't stop jumping up and down.

"That's enough jumping," said Mom.
"'Nuff jumping," agreed Roxy.

"Come on," said Mom.
"Into the stroller
and off we go."

"Off we go," said Roxy. "WHEEEEEE!"

At first, Roxy tried her best to be helpful.
Mom chose things and gave them to Roxy,
and Roxy put them into the grocery cart.

Mom handed Roxy a bag of carrots. "Can you put *these* in the cart, please?" asked Mom.

"*In* the cart!"
said Roxy proudly,
dropping them in.

Then Mom handed Roxy a
big bag of chips.
"In they go!"
said Mom.

"*In* they go!" said Roxy,
squeezing the bag to
make it crackle.

"No squeezing things, Roxy," said Mom. "Do it properly."
"Prop'ly," said Roxy.

Mom handed Roxy a loaf of bread.

"Can you put *this* in the cart, please?" asked Mom.

"*In* the cart!" said Roxy, throwing the bread up in the air.

"No throwing it!" said Mom. "Do it nicely."

"Nicely," agreed Roxy.

Then Mom handed Roxy a can of beans.
Roxy bent down and rolled it along the floor.
"Rolling it!" she said. "Rolling along!"

"Enough!" said Mom. "If you can't help me
properly, you'll have to go in the seat."

"*In* the seat!" said Roxy, grabbing the cart and running off with it.

"COME BACK HERE, ROXY!" shouted Mom. "You'd better stop right now
or there'll be trouble — AND I MEAN IT!"

"You're *not* being very helpful, Roxy," said Mom, plunking her into the cart.

"Not very helpful," agreed Roxy sadly.

Mom headed toward the baked goods aisle.

"Let's get something fun for dessert," she said. "Look, they've got that cake
with the piggy face on it. You like that one, don't you?"

"Like that one!" said Roxy.

"I'll just put it into the cart," said Mom.

Roxy watched the cake go in and twisted around to look at it.

"HOLD the piggy cake?" she asked.

"No, no!" said Mom. "Leave it in the cart. OK? Just leave it."

"Just leave it," agreed Roxy, nodding wisely.

"That's right," said Mom nervously. "Just LEAVE it — OK?"

"Just HOLD it?" Roxy asked again, smiling very sweetly. "Just HOLD the piggy cake."

THEN MOM MADE A BIG MISTAKE.

"All right then," she said, taking the box out of the cart. "Just HOLD it, OK?"

Roxy held out her arms
and wiggled her fingers.

"Just HOLD it," she agreed,
grabbing the box and
clutching it tightly.

"That's right," said Mom.
"Just HOLD it — OK?"

Roxy clutched the cake a bit *too* tightly. Then she looked up at her mom and smiled — a very *determined* smile.

"HAVE the piggy cake!" said Roxy very loudly. "HAVE the piggy cake NOW!" Roxy squeezed the box, and the cake fell out.

"No, NO!" said Mom, trying to grab the cake. "Give the cake to Mommy!"

"HAVE THE PIGGY CAKE!" yelled Roxy. "HAVE THE PIGGY CAKE NOW!"

Mom tried to lift Roxy out of the seat, but Roxy stuck her legs out straight and fell over backward.

Mom tried to grab the cake, but Roxy held on to it. EVERYONE WAS LOOKING!

Finally, Mom wrestled the squashed cake from Roxy's clutches and put what was left of it back into the cart.

Roxy was screaming her head off. "GIVE ME THE PIGGY CAKE! HAVE THE PIGGY CAKE! AAAAAAAH! WANT IT NOW!"

Roxy carried on screaming while Mom paid for the groceries.

"I'm so sorry about this," said Mom to the cashier. "I think
she must be tired. You're not *usually* like this, are you, Roxy?"

But Roxy was plunging headfirst into the back of the cart.
"GIVE ME THE PIGGY CAKE NOW!" she screamed. "AAAAAAH!"

Mom packed the bags as fast as possible, crammed Roxy
into the stroller, and hurried out of the store.

EVERYONE WAS STILL LOOKING.

Roxy went on yelling all the way home.
"GIVE ME THE PIGGY CAKE! AAAAAH! AAAAAH!
WANT IT NOW! AAAAAAAH!"

"ROXY!" said Mom. "For goodness' sake! Everyone's looking at you. Stop that noise at once."

But Roxy didn't stop at once.
In fact, she didn't stop at all
until they got to the front door.

Mom pushed the stroller into the hall and sat down
at the bottom of the stairs.

Roxy was very tired, and Mom was
very annoyed.

"Now then, Roxy," said Mom sternly.
"You were very naughty."

"*Very* naughty," agreed
Roxy sadly.

"So, what do you say
to Mommy?" asked Mom.

Roxy smiled her best, sorriest smile and said in a teeny, tiny voice,

"Have the piggy cake . . .

please?"